WHERE IS THE CAT?

WRITTEN BY MICHÈLE DUFRESNE · ILLUSTRATED BY MAX STASIUK

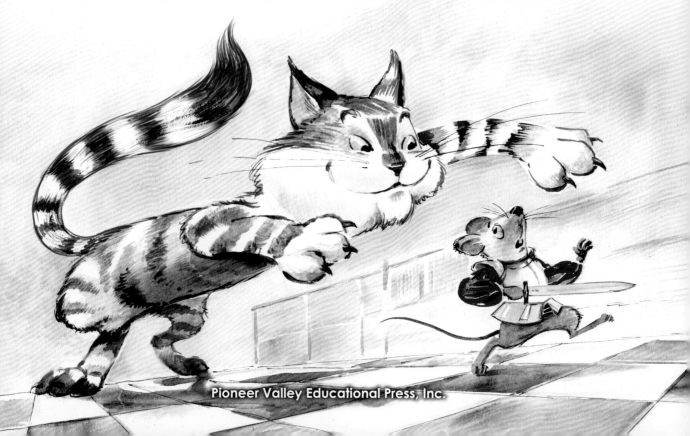

Pioneer Valley Educational Press, Inc.

Is the cat in here?

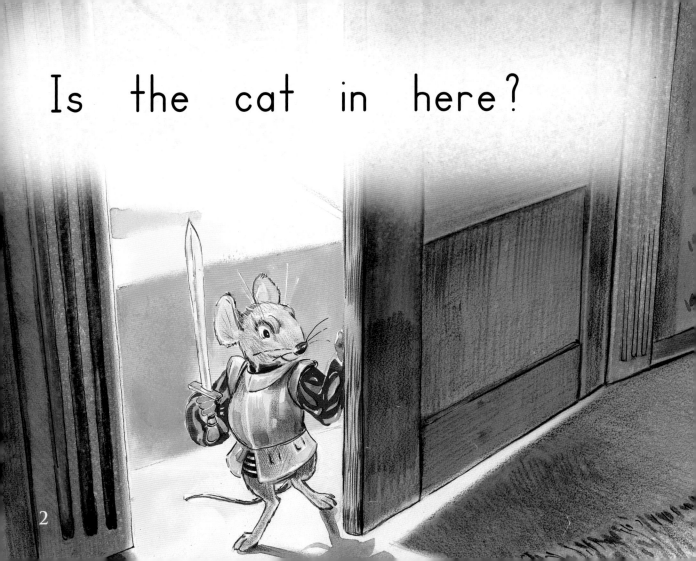

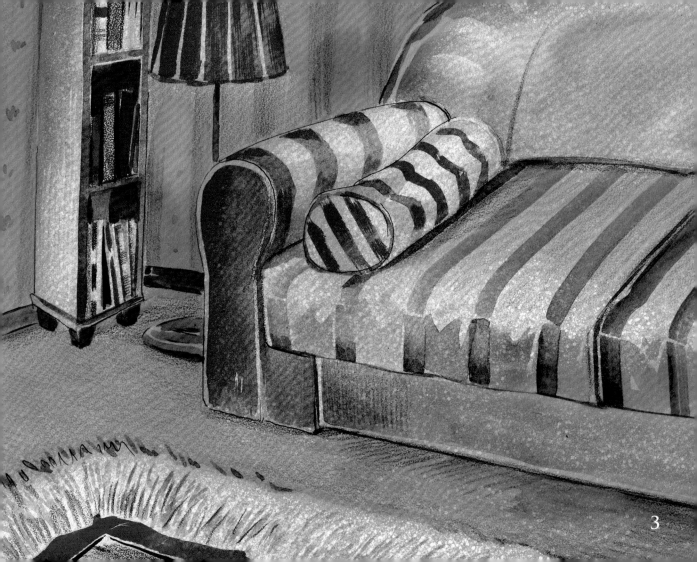

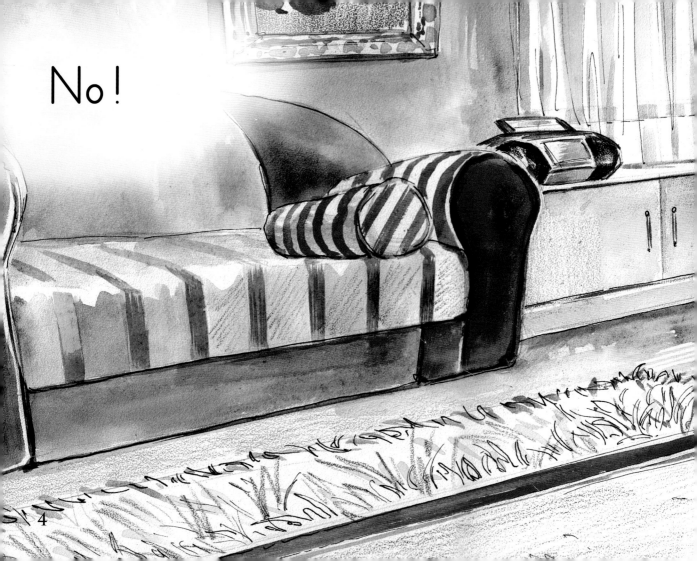

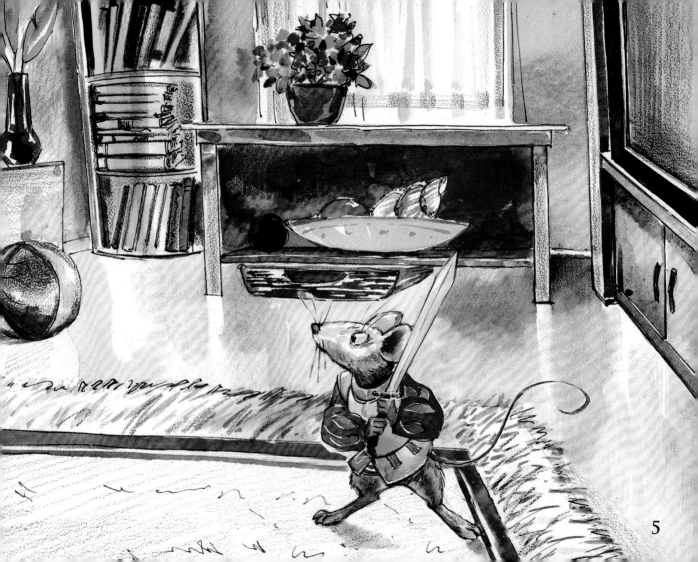

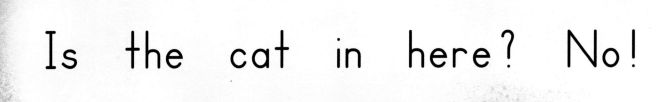

Is the cat in here? No!

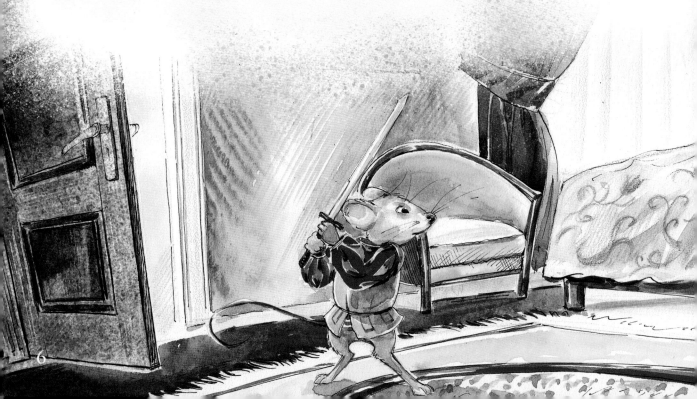

6

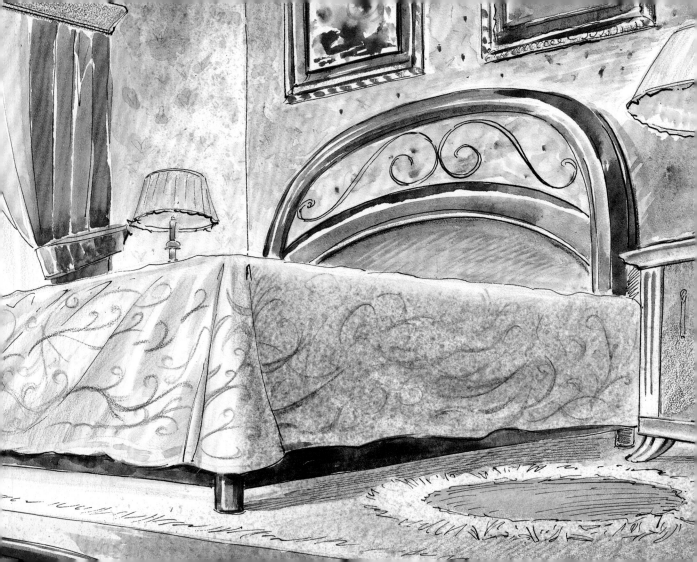

Is the cat in here? No!

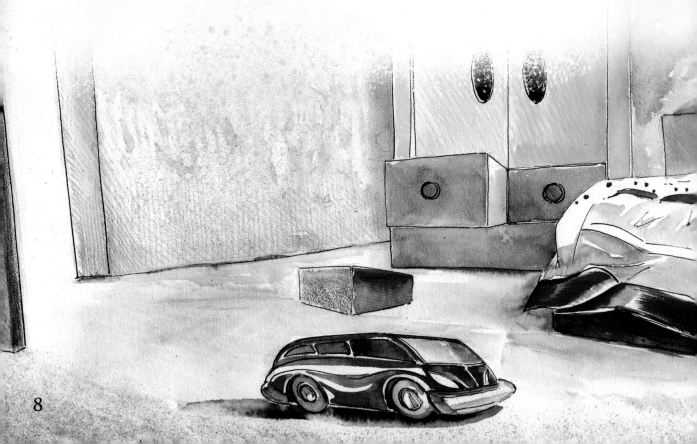

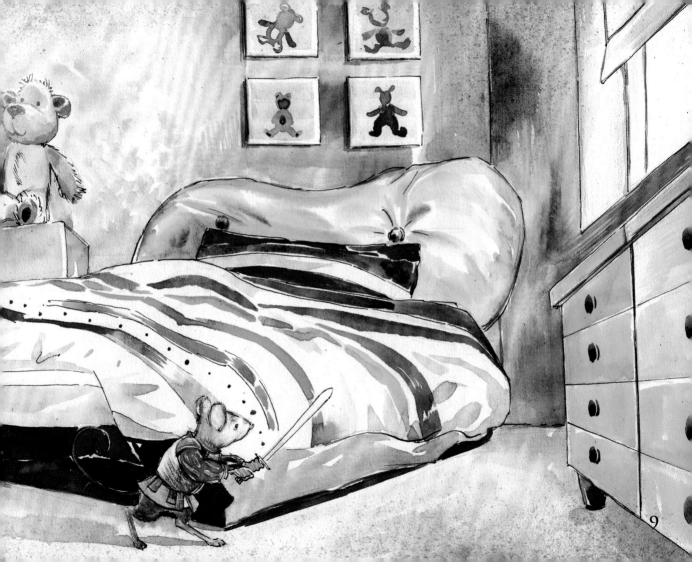

Is the cat in here?

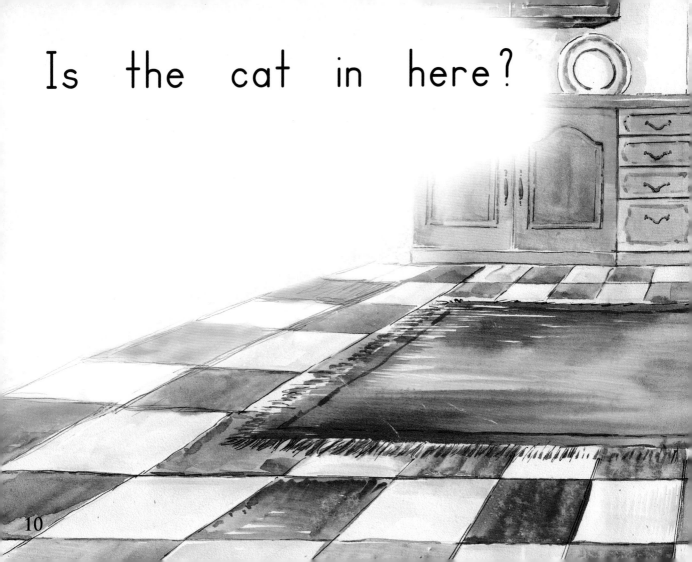

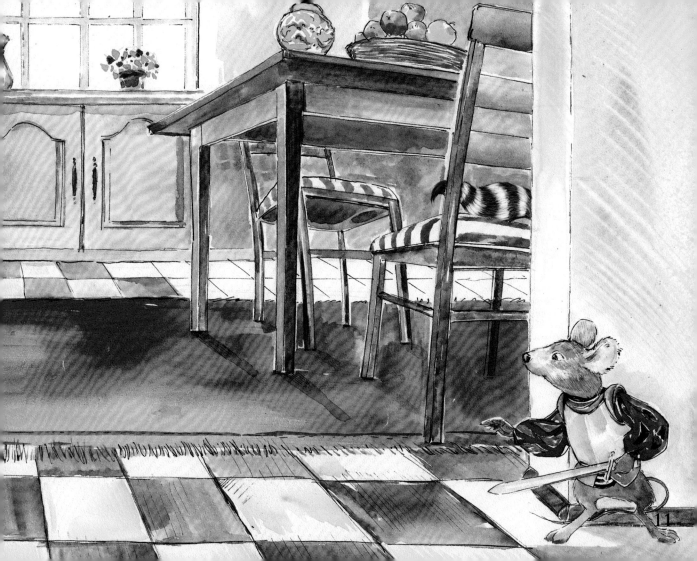

Yes! The cat is in here.

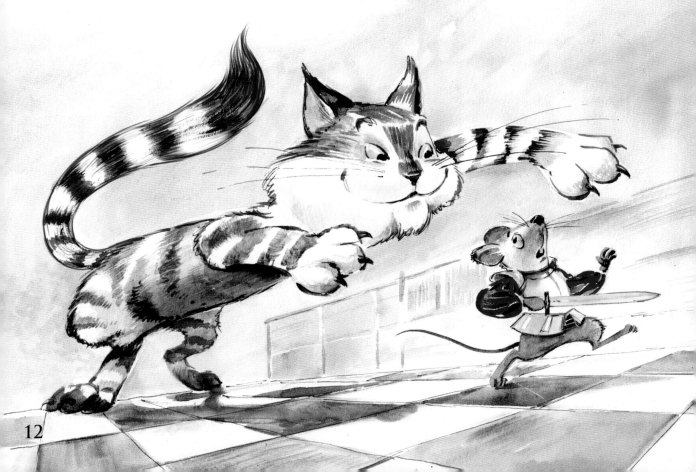